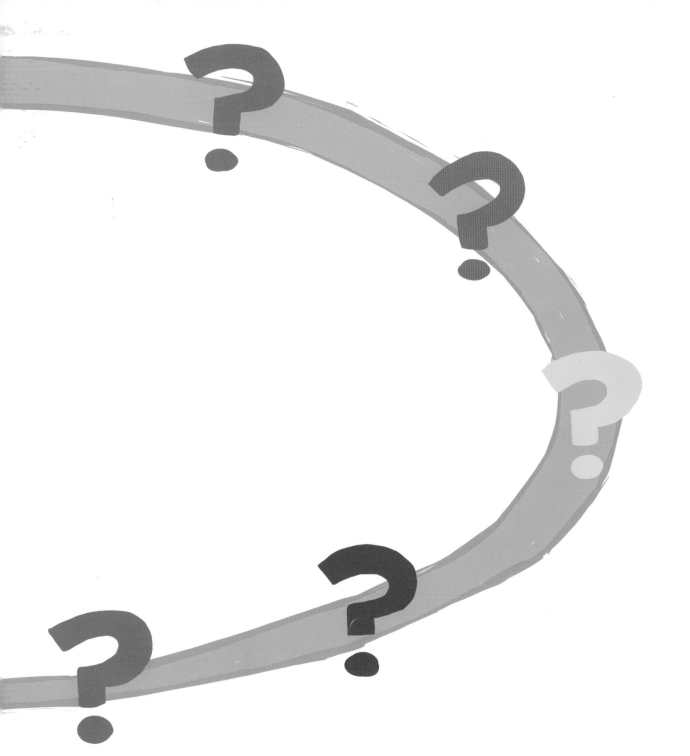

For John, my strong,
dependable Ox
—C. T.

To my good friends
April and Mariah
—M. V.

ATHENEUM BOOKS FOR YOUNG READERS
An imprint of Simon & Schuster Children's Publishing Division • 1230 Avenue of
the Americas, New York, New York 10020 • Text copyright © 2015 by Christian
Trimmer • Illustrations copyright © 2015 by Melissa van der Paardt • All rights
reserved, including the right of reproduction in whole or in part in any form. •
ATHENEUM BOOKS FOR YOUNG READERS is a registered trademark of Simon & Schuster, Inc.
• Atheneum logo is a trademark of Simon & Schuster, Inc. • For information about special
discounts for bulk purchases, please contact Simon & Schuster Special Sales at 1-866-506-1949
or business@simonandschuster.com. • The Simon & Schuster Speakers Bureau can bring authors to your live
event. For more information or to book an event, contact the Simon & Schuster Speakers Bureau at 1-866-248-3049 or visit our website at
www.simonspeakers.com. • Book design by Lauren Rille • The text for this book is set in Burbank. • The illustrations for this book are rendered
digitally. • Manufactured in China • 0915 SCP • First Edition • 10 9 8 7 6 5 4 3 2 1 • Library of Congress Cataloging-in-Publication Data •
Trimmer, Christian. • Mimi and Shu in I'll race you! / Christian Trimmer ; illustrated by Melissa van der Paardt. — First edition. • pages cm
• Summary: Mimi the kitten and Shu the mouse set off on an epic race to win a spot in the Chinese Zodiac—and cupcakes. • ISBN
978-1-4814-2330-4 (hardcover) • ISBN 978-1-4814-2331-1 (eBook) • [1. Astrology, Chinese—Fiction. 2. Animals—Fiction. 3. Racing—
Fiction.] I. Van der Paardt, Melissa, illustrator. II. Title. III. Title: I'll Race You! PZ7.1.T75Mi 2016 • [E]—dc23 • 2015009340

Christian Trimmer

Mimi and Shu in

I'll Race You!

illustrated by
Melissa van der Paardt

Atheneum Books for Young Readers • New York London Toronto Sydney New Delhi

Mimi the Kitten and Shu the Mouse
sprinted along the path with the other animals.
(Snake slithered.)

Shu focused on the race.
Mimi's thoughts were on the end of it.

Shortly, they came upon Dog.
Dog was kind and always in the mood to play.
He was also competition.

But Shu had a plan.
It was a simple plan.

FETCH!

But effective.

As Mimi and Shu continued along the path to the finish line, they ran into other animals.

And each time, Shu,
clever as he was, had a plan.

That is, until they came across Dragon.

Mimi and Shu were making
very good progress.

But then they came upon a river.

Brave Tiger and sweet Rabbit were already
making their way across.
Shu knew he had to think fast.

Just then, hard-working Ox, who happened to be a great swimmer, arrived. Shu rushed over to her.

Mimi promised you could have her cupcake if you let us ride on your back across the river.

Now, despite all evidence, Mimi was eager to
be the first to cross the finish line
(and thus the first to pick a cupcake).
She could easily beat Ox in a foot race,
but Shu was fast **and** clever.
So, for the first time that day,
Mimi came up with a plan.

She would have to push Shu into the river.

But indeed, Shu was fast **and** clever,
and just as Mimi lunged at him . . .

Shu stepped out of the way.

Now, Shu did not feel good about seeing his best friend fall into the river. . . .

But it sure felt good when he was
the first to cross the finish line!

all the cupcakes were gone.

Luckily, she had
the best best friend.

Dog You are loyal and kind (and, every now and then, stubborn).

(1970, 1982, 1994, 2006, 2018, 2029)

Pig You are generous and helpful, but mind the excess!

(1971, 1983, 1995, 2007, 2019, 2030)

Rooster You are confident and trustworthy . . . and a bit of a show-off.

(1969, 1981, 1993, 2005, 2017, 2028)

The
CHINESE

Monkey You are clever, playful . . . and oh so mischievous!

(1968, 1980, 1992, 2004, 2016, 2028)

Goat You are serene and creative . . . and a bit of a loner.

(1967, 1979, 1991, 2003, 2015, 2027)

Horse You are outgoing and funny! Make sure to finish what you start!

(1966, 1978, 1990, 2002, 2014, 2026)

Snake You are intelligent and graceful, but also a tad materialistic.

(1965, 1977, 1989, 2001, 2013, 2025)